A Surprise for Wendy

by Alison Inches
illustrated by Diane Dubreuil

SCHOLASTIC INC.

New York Toronto London Auckland Sydney
Mexico City New Delhi Hong Kong Buenos Aires

HiT™
ENTERTAINMENT

Based upon the television series *Bob the Builder*™
created by HIT Entertainment PLC and Keith Chapman,
with thanks to HOT Animation, as seen on Nick Jr.®

ISBN 0-439-40569-6

12 11 10 9 8 7 6 5 4 3 2 1   2 3 4 5 6 7/0

Printed in the U.S.A.

First Scholastic printing, March 2003

"I am late!" said . WENDY

"And my  is a mess!" GARDEN

"Your  can wait," GARDEN

said . "You have a BOB

train to catch."

 picked up 's .

SCOOP   WENDY   SUITCASE

"Good-bye!" said .

WENDY

"Good-bye!"
said  and .

BOB   DIZZY

"**Meow!**" said .

PILCHARD

"What will we do without ?" asked .

WENDY

DIZZY

"I know! We can surprise  and clean up her 🌸," 😊 said.

WENDY

GARDEN   BOB

"This will be fun!"
said .
DIZZY
"Rock and Roll!"
said .
ROLEY

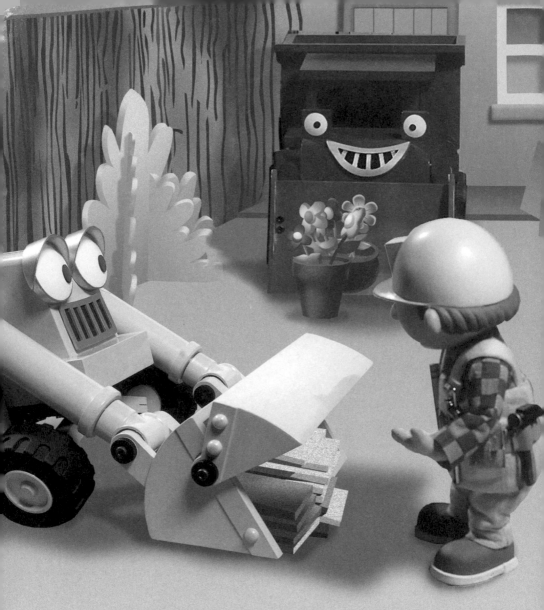

"We have to work fast," said . " will be home by ."

BOB WENDY

SIX O'CLOCK

The machines
got to work.

mixed the 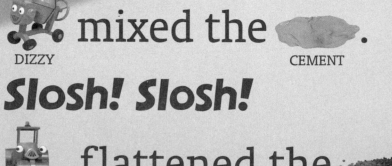.

DIZZY   CEMENT

Slosh! Slosh!

 flattened the .

ROLEY   DIRT

Rumble! Rumble!

 used his .

BOB HAMMER

Bang! Bang!

looked at his .

BOB   WATCH

"We have to work faster!"

he said.

So the machines
worked faster.

Slosh! Slosh!
Rumble! Rumble!
Bang! Bang!

  spread the .

DIZZY

CEMENT

 scooped the .

MUCK

DIRT

 hung the .

LOFTY PLANTER

 planted the .

BOB FLOWERS

Slosh! Slosh!

Rumble! Rumble!

Bang! Bang!

"Hello!"  said.
WENDY
"I am home!" Then
she put down her .
SUITCASE

"I am HOME!" shouted 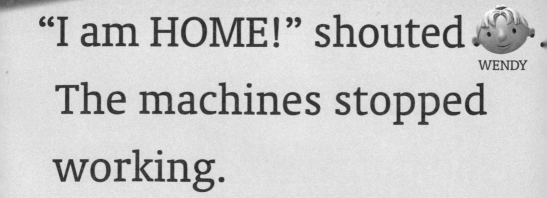 WENDY The machines stopped working.

"Surprise!" said .
BOB

 smiled.

WENDY

"My !" she said.

GARDEN

"**Did we fix it?**"
asked .
SCOOP
"**Yes, you did!**" said .
WENDY

"My new  is perfect," said .

GARDEN

WENDY

"Hooray!" said .

BOB

"Thank you!" said .

WENDY